MAX

Weekly Reader Children's Book Club presents

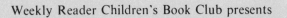

MAX

story & pictures by
Rachel Isadora

MACMILLAN PUBLISHING CO., INC.
New York
COLLIER MACMILLAN PUBLISHERS
London

Macmillan Publishing Co., Inc.
866 Third Avenue, New York, N.Y. 10022
Collier Macmillan Canada, Ltd.
Printed in the United States of America
Library of Congress Catalog Card Number: 76-9088
ISBN 0-02-747450-7

Weekly Reader Children's Book Club Edition

For my parents
and Grandfather Max

With special thanks to
Libby, Alan,
and of course, Brian

Max is a great baseball player. He can run fast, jump high, and hardly ever misses a ball. Every Saturday he plays with his team in the park.

On Saturday mornings he walks with his sister Lisa to her dancing school. The school is on the way to the park.

One Saturday when they reach the school, Max still has lots of time before the game is to start. Lisa asks him if he wants to come inside for a while.

Max doesn't really want to, but he says O.K. Soon the class begins. He gets a chair and sits near the door to watch.

The teacher invites Max
to join the class, but he must
take off his sneakers first.

He stretches at the barre.

He tries to do the split.

And the pas de chat. He is having fun.

Just as the class lines up to do leaps across the floor,
Lisa points to the clock. It is time for Max to leave.

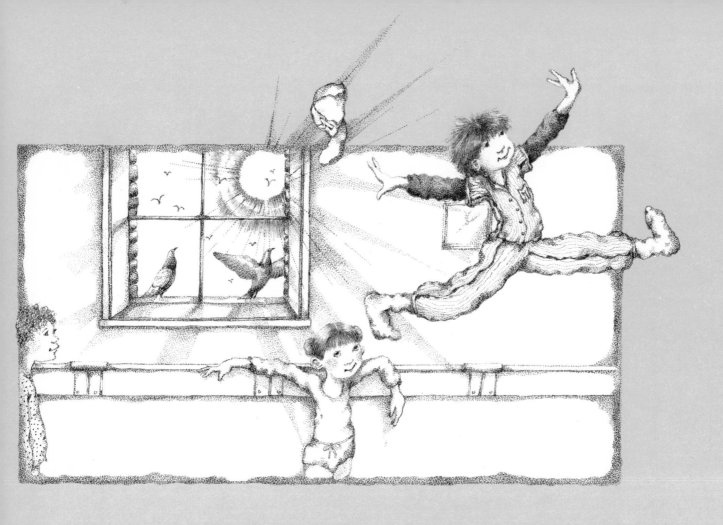

Max doesn't want to miss the leaps. He waits and takes his turn.

Then he must go.

He leaps all the way to the park.

He is late. Everybody is waiting for him.

He goes up to bat.

Strike one!

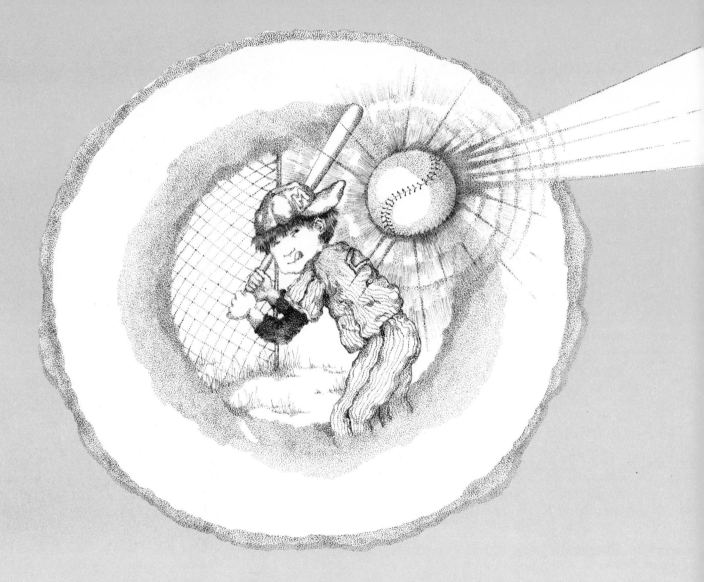

He tries again.

Strike two!

And then...

A home run!

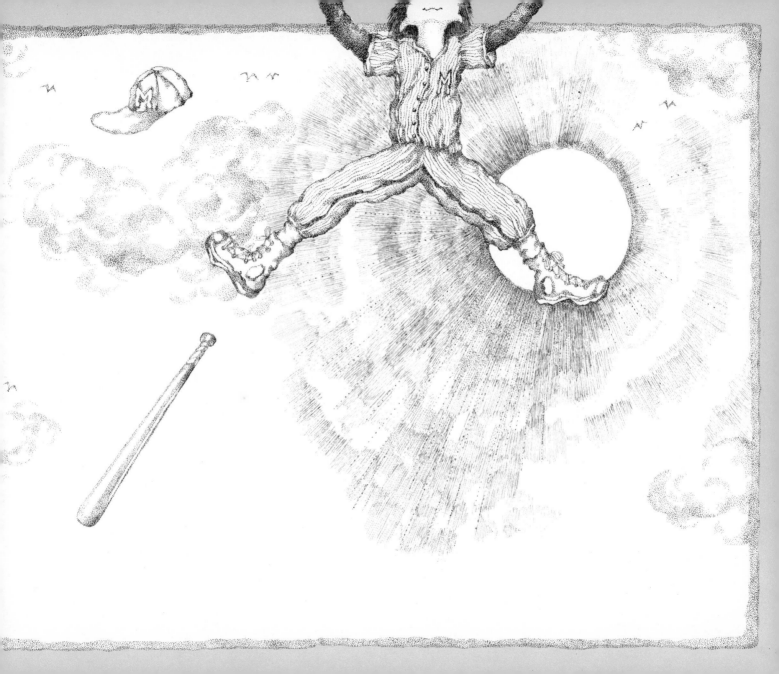

Now Max has a new way to warm up for the game on Saturdays.
He goes to dancing class.